POSTHUMOUS
Love story

Juan Manuel Rodríguez Caamaño

Posthumous
Juan Manuel Rodríguez Caamaño

First edition October 2019
First published Mexico City, October 2019

POSTHUMOUS
Love story

Juan Manuel Rodríguez Caamaño

I received that hot July 28, 2018 a strange package addressed to me, with the exact address of my house, even with that detail of the letter B at the end that many confused with the address next door with the same number and only people I knew nearby, but from a seemingly unknown recipient, so before opening it I called the parcel company to object that the name of the person who sent it was strange and I wanted to know what it contained. With the high rates of insecurity in Coatzacoalcos we were all paranoid about any probable extortion. They told me that the envelope contained an invitation, probably to an event but they had no more information about it. All these formal parties sometimes use a parcel service to send their invitations to all their foreign guests. The detail in this case is that that name did not sound to me in the least: William Ernesto Torruco Stackpole, maybe he was a distant relative, my father had ten brothers and they all lived in the north of the country, so maybe it was some distant cousin or husband of some cousin or niece of mine.

I opened it, more out of curiosity than for being interested in a probable party, anyway I thought to call the sender to tell him that he had been wrong of recipient if there was a contact phone in the invitation, maybe there was some other guy with my name and they were confused to get their address.

I was amazed at the size and elegance of that dark envelope, perhaps the most sumptuous I had ever seen, I did not know wealthy families and it was not my fascination to do so, so I imagined that it was a mistake that shipment. It did not seem like a wedding or quinceañera, because in the center it brought an image that I did not know sealed, it was like the shield of some aristocratic family, of those who love to presume that they have royalty blood. It also had some initials but without the conjunction "and" which made me doubt that they were the initials of a couple for their nuptial bond, "Z S". I was going to open it a thunderous noise scared me and prevented me from finding out what the reason for that invitation was. I had left the kitchen window open and a strong wind threw away some of the dirty dishes that I had used that day. My heart was beating fast, agitated by that fright that fortunately only remained in.

I took care of lifting that dump and seeing an ice-cold beer in the refrigerator I uncovered it and drank it while listening to music and preparing something simple for dinner. I was almost asleep when I remembered the subject of the invitation received in the morning, so I took the envelope and went to my bed to open it while writing down the last earrings of the next day.

The Torruco Inzunsa family

Is pleased to invite you to his daughter's funerals:

Zaida Sofia Torruco Inzunza

They will be held in the city of Culiacan, Sinaloa on July 29 and 30, 2018 in the gardens of the Torruco Insunza residence, located at kilometer 117 of the federal highway.

Please confirm your attendance at 687-687-2777Flight

Code PJ54017ADO

Ticket # 3567

Hotel Sinaloa Room 127

Amazing! I did not know of the existence of invitations to a funeral, it seemed to me perhaps something of bad taste, but I imagine in the aristocratic families it was common. I have never heard those names in my life, but no surname was known to me. I did a very brief search in the internet search engines, in my social networks, I inquired with all my acquaintances of the university since I had several foreign friends in the career when I studied in Monterrey, maybe it was the family of some former colleague that I did not remember. We graduated one hundred and fifty-six students. It was difficult to remember everyone's names, but no, nobody knew how to give me reason for those names. When I read the invitation again because of the incessant curiosity of seeing more details about it, I finally observed a confirmation phone and a flight code prepared to travel the next day from Veracruz to Mexico City and from there to Culiacan. Including the transfer by land by bus from Coatzacoalcos to the port of Veracruz. I was struck by so much concern in detail for me to attend the funeral of someone I did not know. I asked my friends based in Culiacan if they knew that family and they told me that it was a well-known family in the state, they were dedicated to export cotton, which was one of the main industries of the city.

I checked early to try to confirm that I would not attend and even inform them that I had no idea who the deceased person was and probably they were wrong, her father answered me and without letting me talk he told me with great enthusiasm that Zaida had wished that I was there .

- Juan Manuel, what a pleasure to greet you! My daughter talked a lot about you, we would very much like you to join us.

I was so sad to tell him that I didn't even know her and at such insistence on his part I agreed to attend her funerals, or I know what I was thinking but sensitivity has always overcome me.

I did not dislike a three-day vacation with all expenses paid, besides I could take the opportunity to relax and finish a novel that I had pending to publish. So, I packed my black suit and dark tie and confirmed my transport from Coatzacoalcos to Veracruz, but not before calling my job to ask for permission to leave for a week. It was a time of low demand, so the work at that time was not so exhaustive. And even more that I was a member of that microenterprise and could give me certain privileges.

The transport was direct to the Veracruz airport, so I just had to wait a few hours to board and reach my final destination, I decided to sleep on that route because reading on the road caused me a headache.

Arriving at the Culiacan airport, a luxurious black sedan car was waiting to take me to Zaida's house, located on the outskirts of the city, almost an hour away. In that period, I barely stole some words from the driver, he seemed to enjoy doing his job and did not like being interrupted even to socialize a little. Even so, I was able to find out a little more about that mysterious family I was about to meet. He confirmed that the head of the family was dedicated to planting cotton that was the main industry of that small municipality of Sinaloa on the outskirts of Culiacan. Apparently Zaida Sofia was an only child and had died of lung cancer just at 38 years of age, very young, it must be a very painful loss contrary to the calm and jovial attitude of her father when I talked for a few minutes on the phone with him. I asked the driver, his name was Fernando and he dressed very elegant all in black, he showed me a recent photo of her, and he replied very rude that he should have one if he was just the driver.

Finally, fortunately we arrived at our destination, the heat was no longer as intense as in Culiacan and I only wanted to fulfill the involuntarily acquired commitment and take the opportunity to visit places around. When we arrived at that mansion, it was full of visitors, all very elegant in black, some in bows and others in ties, to celebrate the funeral of that mysterious woman in my life who must have been very dear to that community. I looked for the parents of the deceased to offer my condolences and stay with them for a while, the line to do so was very long so I chose to pour myself a coffee in the kitchen of the house in which the wait was lightened, it was a delight that drink, as rich as that of my Veracruz land, I would almost swear it was from Coatepec.

I went out to the beautiful and immense garden full of bougainvillea, jacarandas and very large and thick trees. I needed to remove some fresh air and I began to talk with her relatives about trivial things.

- The garden is beautiful.

- Yes, it was one of Zaida's passions to take care of it every day even when you see it so beautiful, when she lived it looked even more splendid and colorful.

- It must be, the plants also feed on the affection one seeks for them.

- It even seems that I'm listening to her, excuse me, are you?

- Juan Manuel, I'm glad to come from Veracruz.

- Nice to meet you, Juan Manuel, I am Fernanda and he is my husband Alejandro, Frida was my cousin, where did you know her?

That question put me in a big predicament, so I had to invent something credible.

- We study university together.

- In Monterrey or in Boston?

- In Monterrey.

The conversation continued fortunately without touching the issue of how my relationship with her was. They spoke wonders of Zaida each one, for a moment I wished I had met her in life and to personally enjoy some of the qualities they exhibited. We talked almost half an hour until I had to go to the bathroom of so much coffee, the closest was in the study of the house, there I could see numerous pictures of her with her father. I had not noticed how beautiful she was, in most of her photos on social networks she uploaded places she visited and her pets but very rarely published photos of her, and from afar where her fine features, her golden hair and that natural smile that radiated happiness. But there in the intimacy of her home there were photos of her very closely in many landscapes and one or another painting by a famous painter who had eternalized her in oils. In that painting under a maple tree she wore a spectacular smile, with the snow contrasting with the brightness of her hair, I thought about the tree and the snow, that was Canadian territory, I did not know Canada.

How sad that a woman so beautiful and with a lifetime ahead has left to exist, and still could not decipher what was her relationship with me. I continued to be charmed in that room looking at all her memories, I had the time of the world, I had only come to comply with giving condolences to the bereaved and from there I was free of any compromise, I imagined drinking a beer maybe on the beach of Mazatlán, a from the most famous beaches of Sinaloa and Mexico, or a wine from the hotel overlooking the sea. I checked the books that were in the study and that she supposedly read, I was surprised that we had the same adoration for the Argentine writer Jorge Luis Borges, they were all his stories on the main shelf. I could also find some authors that I did not know from all over the world, Japanese, Swedish, Finnish.

I was stunned to check her library and find all the copies of my works as a writer. I was not very famous; I was rather an amateur and freelance writer who enjoyed expressing all the ideas that came to my mind and my works were available on the internet and were rarely sold. That is why it caught my attention so much that she had my entire collection of stories, none was missing. I opened my favorite, "Always you," and if I was astonished to see her on her shelf, when I saw that she was signed by me, I was shocked, I didn't remember at first instance any presentation of that book. I should have signed it in my bookstore. I checked the dedication to try to remember, but that was the strangest thing, I usually put the classic "with all my affection", and my signature. But this one had a very peculiar dedication.

For Zaida Sofia:

"My most beautiful admirer, the one of the unmistakable smile miles away."

A dedication and such a beautiful woman, I would remember them and yet I couldn't do it. The dedication of

"Yesterday" made it even more obvious that I had met her and that I had really autographed her books personally.

For Zaida Sofia:

"With all my affection, I hope you enjoy this story that I personally love.

P.S. As much as I love your smile, thank you for allowing me to meet it today." 02/15/2016

In theory I had few years of having met her, and it seemed that she had been present in my few book presentations. I began to remember and I remembered that I only made a presentation of "Yesterday" and as it was in my hometown there were many people, some only attended for friendship rather than because they were fans of my work; others, friends of my parents and sisters, out of commitment. How could I not remember that beautiful woman, my memory almost never failed. I checked in the other novels if they had a dedication but no. They were the only ones, which for a moment excused me from forgetting her because those that were autographed had been the most popular presentations and for example "Psicoaffaire" which had been my first novel and of which I only did a small private event. I had my signature.

I stuck in a photo album of her that was on the desk. It could not be true, the place I always wanted to visit, the

Dutch gardens full of tulips, with her golden skin, her splendid smile, her young face full of freckles that fascinate me, her imposing look and that colorful background that only Amsterdam has in spring.

I always wanted to be there.

Her medical degree with all her classmates, she had to graduate for the same years as me, was a beautiful ritual where she showed her beauty even covered with that gown. And I told her cousin that I had studied college with her, and I didn't have even the slightest notion of medicine, the good thing was that we didn't delve into it.

Each of the places I always dreamed of knowing and that to date had been impossible for reasons of money, time or health, appeared along that gallery of portraits of her in the studio. How lucky she was in life to be able to enjoy places that I described in my novels and that I never knew as the region of Galicia in "Always you".

She had photos in Corunna and Compostela. Very sheltered, it is seen that it was a very cold area in winter, maybe she had been able to travel and enjoy the landscapes of the route that the protagonist makes with Brais from Madrid to La Coruña, which I invented in my mind.

That photo in the obelisk of Buenos Aires made me imagine that I was traveling there and as in my novel of "Aleph: The Myth", I was looking for that place where for Borges in his science fiction story that space was located from where you could see everything in the universe. And I felt something curious, I imagined that I was looking for it with her by my side as a great friend supporting me to decipher that enigma.

I was surprised to see that sea in the background in that photo in the center of the room, that dark blue sea with the reflection of a radiant sun and in the background a hill with a majestic sunset, I knew it. It was my hometown, Coatzacoalcos. She was there, surely it was when the presentation of one of my autographed books, I would not find another option to visit my city located in the remote Southeast state. It broke my soul to see her prostrated in that picture in the bed of a hospital, probably from her last moments, with her family and that elegant dressed man and with whom I think she married in the clinic. All were very elegant and toasted with a bottle of champagne, despite the hard moment it seemed, she did not lose that incredible smile that appeared naturally in all the paintings.

She also had a photo on that historic bridge in Prague, one on the Malecon in Montevideo and others in the cathedral of Florence, which reminded me of the places I imagined when I wrote my novels of the "Prague Dance", "Aleph: The Myth" and "Planet Gois."

And just when I was closely touching those photos hanging on the wall, I jumped from the fright that his father gave me when he touched my back.

- What are you doing, son?

- Nothing, I was just watching some photos of Zaida Sofia.

- Yes, I understand, it's horrible to miss her. You have no idea what hurt me when I learned the news of her illness. I did everything in my power to keep her here, even after her death I would do anything to make her proud of her father.

- I know, although I didn't have much contact with her, the news still hurts in my soul, believe me.

- I know, son, you don't have to explain anything to me, I know how you feel, hurt by ... - He interrupted me by raising his hand just at the height of my mouth.

- You don't have to show me anything, I know perfectly your relationship with my Zai.

- Is that, although it was not a very ... - Again, with that gesture my lips shut up again.

- I know all about your relationship.

I did not know what to say, for a moment I thought that this old man had the feeling that between Zaida Sofia and

I there was something romantic which was not true. I could feel it in his way of expressing it.

- I guarantee you, sir, that it was only a relationship of friends' sir, in fact it was a distance friendly relationship.

He let out a laugh that could be heard even in the hallways of the house where there were also visitors to the funeral.

- Now you have stolen the first laugh since Zai left me. I know! I know what your relationship was, I know why you are here. I sent you that envelope at my daughter's request. One of her wills before she died was that, that you were here today at her farewell.

I was shocked by those revelations of her father, I didn't know what to say, I had so many emotions at the time that I didn't know how to behave. In fact, that man had done everything possible for me to be there. He personally had confirmed my attendance and scheduled my trip and my lodging.

It is seen that Zaida Sofía was his entire life, his only daughter, the way he expressed herself and all the photos with her that I saw in the study of the house, showed that she was his reason for living. He asked me to accompany him to sit near where her body was while attending to the people who arrived.

The visitors saw me with good eyes after a little happiness in him at that terrible moment for Mr. Torruco was living. The sleepless night, which looked very sad upon my arrival, became more bearable with the change of attitude of Zaida's father, was the leader of a family of eight brothers and one of the most recognized cotton entrepreneurs in the world, and proudly Mexican. He told me great anecdotes with his daughter and his way of describing her, although parents always speak wonders of their children, it was extraordinary.

The most rugged moment of the trip arrived and the saddest one I had lived in my life, the moment of the burial. The pain of the bereaved to know that it is the last time they will have a close eye on the loved one is so heartbreaking that it infects everyone present and crying is inevitable, mine was just as heartbreaking as that of any close relative. I turned around to understand why I felt so sad and, in all eyes, I found that same sadness. Her father gave me a white rose to drop on her coffin, I tried to reject it, but it was impossible for me before the old man's insistent gaze. I took between my fingers that beautiful rose that looked as full of life as she did in each of her photos and threw it watching how it fell almost in slow motion on that coppery coffin. I imagined within that box a smile from her towards me when I made that last gift from me and I felt extremely good, it was a ritual that I had always considered unnecessary, but at that moment I understood the reason for it.

We returned to that beautiful mansion to drink coffee and tea with all the relatives, while all the attendees talked beautiful anecdotes with the beautiful absent, I preferred a peppermint tea, my favorite since I left so much coffee because it altered me too much and caused me gastritis. What delicious herbal tea I tried in that house, I even kept the bag that contained it to look for that brand that looked very elegant later in a supermarket and try it in my house with the sunset of my land.

We said goodbye to the last guest, Mr. Torruco treated me as if I was one more child and we continued drinking tea when the last relatives hugged Don Ernesto and left the house. After an hour, only he and I stayed in the room where hours before had been the body of Zaida Sofia.

- You'll wonder, what are you doing here?

- Yes, something like that, the truth is that this situation has me very confused.

- I will be direct with you, my daughter and I had no secrets, since she was a child, she was the most important thing for me in life. I dedicated myself to work day and night with the sole purpose that she will never lack anything and that she would be immensely happy always. One day she told me that I didn't have to work so much, that her happiness didn't depend on the gifts I could give her but on being with me all the time. That's how since she was in high school, she started working with me and we spent not only time at home all as a family, but apart we made an excellent team. She was the brightest I've ever met at work, took us to unimaginable places, to be competitive worldwide. Her dedication made her focus on her work day and night and never gave time for love. There came a time when I begged her to find someone to not be alone when her mother and I were gone. What irony we are still here, and she is gone. But well that's history, one day I told her that I wanted her to meet the son of a partner who since he saw her for the first time was taken by her, they met and he fell in love, how could he not do it if Zai was perfect, but she kept thinking only about her father, her mother and her job, no matter how much I made her see that to start a family she didn't need to be madly in love, that a marriage is more than a love relationship, it's a team relationship, neither she listened but tried to have a relationship with that suitor and so they lasted for years. Until the last moment she agreed to make him happy joining in marriage a month before her departure. That was her apparent life story, but there was something more than just her and I knew. She was passionate about reading and sometimes I didn't understand why, she told me that I could live a thousand lives reading thousands of books. And it's true because that made her immensely happy. One day traveling to Cancun we stopped on the side of the road at the height of Veracruz in a self-service store and saw on a shelf a book with a cover and a title that caught her attention. That strange title that had never occurred to her led her to ask for its author.

- He is a local author, miss, you see that here in Veracruz we are all poets like Agustín Lara.

- Ok, give me a copy, we'll see how the Veracruz people write.

And he laughed as he turned to see me. Before arriving at the next booth, she had already read more than half of the book, she did not pay attention the next couple of hours because she was delighted with that text. The last hours of the trip were to tell me the tragic story of Juan Martín and Carolina. She told me with so much emotion and detail that she thought she could get to love someone, what happened was that she hasn't found someone to make her vibrate like in the book. She told me that she would search the internet for more information about the author and was excited to know that a second part of this story already existed, and she immediately asked for it. She also acquired all the books written by that freelance writer who wrote for pleasure, for the love of letters as he said in his biography. And that is how she fell in love with each story of that author, even though they were of different genres, each book was marking her life and feeling on many occasions that it matched the characters of your imagination. So, I asked her to do something about it and she decided to meet you. She went to one of your presentations and told me that you flirted. A year later, at the second presentation she attended, that flirting was more direct, but she never approached because she already had a commitment but especially because she had just known her destiny with that undesirable disease. Your "Yesterday" novel moved her and made her believe that she could at some time live that story and meet you in the past, but that was not possible. - His voice broke in that part of her story, but he took a breath and drank a little more coffee to continue. - Sometimes I wondered excitedly if someone could fall in love with someone else just by reading their words, just enjoying their talent. And it was when I said: daughter that is love! Love is not something physical, it is not a state of mind, love is to enjoy the things that another person creates in your mind and what makes you feel. And then she sentenced me with two words: I am in love! From that moment she followed your steps as a writer and read again and again each of your works of which she was fascinated by all, she became your main admirer. When she learned that she didn't have much time to live, she made me promise that I would contact you so that you could fulfill her will after she died.

At that moment his crying no longer allowed him to continue telling me how it was that I had appeared in the lives of such excellent people.

- If I hadn't come to the funeral, how would I have known all that?

- If you had not come, I would have looked for you and found the ideal moment to let you know all this. - His crying became deeper - I would have done whatever it was because she lived, I tried everything humanly possible to overcome that disease but not I succeeded, so when she told me what her last will was, I told her that I would not rest until I fulfilled it.

- And what was her last will?

- First that you were here on the day of her farewell, which you have already fulfilled and second that you follow the instructions that she left me on some sheets that she filled in forming a book to which she titled “Posthumous”. Here it is, I give it to you, and I beg you to read it and help me fulfill your dream. You can use everything you need; I'll be there to get it.

- I would be sorry to abuse her predilection for my literature, on the contrary, I should be flattered to have such an admirer, I should be indebted to her.

- You said it, if you think you are indebted to her, she only fulfills her posthumous indications, with that you would make her immensely happy wherever she is, in fact you do not know how happy she was when I told her that I would convince you how it would take place for you to do it, I could die easy. Juanma please help us.

That story broke my heart and even more to know that my words had the power to make someone happy.

- But I don't even know what I should do.

- So, read it all first and then we decide what to do, but please think about it very well.

- Don't worry, I will.

I arrived at the hotel tired, but I uncovered a bottle of wine, sat on the terrace feeling the heat of the Sinaloa summer and began to read.

"Now I can tell you so many things that I could not live, like that I love that look that you have combined between tender and at the same time mysterious, I remember when you autographed "Always Her" you almost ate me with that look. However, I loved feeling your eyes on me, it will read very sickly, but I even imagined having you completely on top of me haha, the things that one writes when it is no longer present. I don't know what the beyond is like but I'm almost sure I'll be seeing that laugh of yours as I read this."

And so it was, I burst out laughing when I met her confessions, how I didn't know it before, maybe we could be great friends, I continued reading excitedly.

"So many things we could do together, but we both had commitments at that time and I was always very respectful of it. Also imagine if so just by reading you I was completely in love with your words, if I had known you capable I would go crazy for you. Or maybe you were better writing and already knowing you I was disappointed in you haha, who knows, you never know what could happen, but we can no longer find out. Something that I loved about your novels were your poems that are necessarily related in each story, your stories are splendid but the poems are perfect, I could

almost swear that each one of them wrote it at a very special moment and for a very special person and in each novel you tried to force a relationship with the feeling of the protagonist, maybe I am wrong but otherwise, I think that as your most fierce admirer I have to tell you ¡Busted! hahahaha."

She stole a laugh again, now more thunderous. Someone had never even hinted at me like that, she had once again noticed something that everyone does not know about my way of writing, I felt no pain of being discovered because that innocent secret she had taken it to the grave. As a child I wrote stanzas, I was fascinated by poetry but when I grew up, I was thinking that nobody was passionate about poetry, that everyone is currently looking for stories, novels but that fewer and fewer people are interested in creating beautiful verses. So the way I decided to make my little library of poems written by me in special moments known was introducing them in my publications, so I tried to make that insertion very subtle so that no one could perceive it, but she did it, it was the only one until now.

"Since we could not live happily together, my last will and what I hope you can fulfill is that we have it posthumously. For this I have left you these indications, so that you know everything you will do and need. Obvious any life plan together, I had to build on the places where you wrote those beautiful stories that were the ones that joined us. So we will start in Buenos Aires

where you and I will go to find the Aleph of Borges, as you did in a fictional way in your novel "Aleph: The myth" I knew from your biography that you were never in Buenos Aires, nor in Montevideo to write "Kiam", neither in Prague that inspired "The dance of Prague", nor in Florence to create "Divine" and yet you developed some fabulous stories with those places, imagine what you and I will do when you can smell the mate and the wine Argentine with your own senses. Imagine what we will do on the boardwalk in Montevideo, how we will get drunk with Becherovka in Prague or how we will virtually marry in the cathedral of Florence. On each sheet with the name of each city come the indications of what we will do together, because I want you to know that at every moment I will be there by your side. My last will is that you immortalize us in a novel, the novel in this story that began from the day you received that package with the news that I had died and you didn't even remember me. I have an unmistakable smile as you expressed in your dedication, and did you forget about me? Hehe don't believe it; I know you must meet thousands of fans of your novels. However, this will be the best novel because it is a true story, however strange it may seem. So, don't wait any longer, start our first trip."

It was surprising to me how she could guess everything about me, even that I would forget that moment when I met her.

Buenos Aires, Argentina. August 1, 2018

The city fascinated me more than I had thought, it had an unequaled architecture, walking through the port with that cold wind of late winter burning my cheeks slightly, it was a sensation that I had not experienced before even living a storm in the month of August, this is possible in the Southern Cone.

The indications were very precise: first day, take a city tour and take a photo in each of the places where she was also. A photo in the obelisk with the same angle facing west to be able to superimpose my image and hers and digitally create an image together in this same place although at different times.

"Surely you will be thinking the same as me, you do not understand why it is such a symbolic monument for the city, when I do not see any quality. No joke as we Mexicans say. Indeed, that was the first thing I thought, having so many beautiful places like the Teatro Colón, why I would have chosen such a simple place, but hey, our image together made it important, maybe some reader of your novel can get us out of doubt about why is such an incipient monument important for a country."

The second day I had to go to a typical place in Buenos Aires, the one that gives its name to one of the most popular soccer teams on the planet, I went to the picturesque neighborhood of La Boca and obviously to the "Boca Juniors" stadium. It seems that she had read enough of me, and she knew it was a dream to know that emblematic site.

"I don't like football at all, but I know that in this place I would have felt a great emotion to feel your heart beating from the pleasure of being here, in the cathedral of soccer for Argentines. Legend has it that to choose the color the team uniform decided at random that it would be the color of the flag of the first ship that entered the port at that time and it was a Swedish ship that gave the team color."

The third day, perhaps the one that motivated me the most because it was the biggest pleasure for me, eating. The richest banquet I've ever had in my life was in Puerto Madero, watching the boats come in and listening to the sounds of the sea. Tasting the roast, the chinchulines, the black pudding and drinking Mendoza wine. The photo there made me feel that I was hugging her standing in the port, I asked some tourists to take it to take care of every detail.

"You cannot stop trying the chinchulines, they are the part that in Mexico we know as gut, but God will know, how they cook it there that has a totally different and unmissable flavor."

The fourth day was the most important.

You get off at the last station of the subway, in the Plaza de la Constitución. You walk on Alvear street and in the corner to your left leaving by the North part of the station you will find a cafeteria called Lucero. Order a Borges style espresso. Write on a napkin if the day is rainy or sunny. And give it to the waiter.

I did everything as is. In my stay in Buenos Aires a drop of water had not fallen, but coincidentally when I was about to take the first sip of my espresso the day became cloudy and it began to rain heavily. So, I wrote on a napkin that the day was rainy and I gave it to the waiter, I felt a little stupid but I would do anything for that woman who admired my words and I began to admire hers too much. The waiter brought me another espresso and told me it was courtesy of the house and handed me an envelope with my name, that really surprised me.

"I love rainy days in Buenos Aires, they are ideal for a cut espresso like the one you are drinking but you must accompany it with dulce de leche, the most typical of the pampas, I agree with you as in your novel: how sad that where the Aleph is located there is now a large warehouse of a commercial chain of groceries. Take advantage and go to the same place where you found the Aleph, there you will find the real Aleph, not that which you romantically found in your novel, but the one that can be savored, at that height on a shelf of that supermarket should be my milk sweets favorites, those of the yellow squares "vauquita", take the first box and return to taste them with another espresso. Do not worry,

in the cafeteria they will not tell you anything to take them, I have already fixed that."

I was beginning to think that Zai had powers to solve everything in life and even after it, she had also put a raincoat inside that envelope so it wouldn't get wet. Even so, water was draining when I entered the place, went down the stairs and located where the dulce de leche was that she liked so much. I took the box and when I moved it, I saw under it a number that was very familiar to me in the first instance: 180447. I drank espresso all afternoon and waited for the night to fall, I ended up like five bars of dulce de leche.

Montevideo, Uruguay. August 6, 2018

I took a ferry from Buenos Aires to Montevideo in the morning, three more hours of travel, I asked for a bottle of wine to lessen that landscape, at first beautiful, of the sea, but then monotonous kilometers and kilometers of that grayish brown color of the sea of La Plata and nothing else around, my mind began to betray me after living those beautiful moments in Buenos Aires. Will I be falling in love with a woman that no longer exists? I arrived in Montevideo and the directions were very simple, enjoy a sunset on that beautiful boardwalk and our photo there feeling what the protagonists of "Kiam" felt, that novel I wrote when they broke my heart for the first time.

"Baptize a star for us, one that only you and I can see each night, choose a name that reminds you of this story we are living. I didn't break my head, creative writer."

The first thing that came to mind when I saw the starry sky reflected in the sea was the smile of "Zai".

P.S. Surely you are so uncreative that you put my name. How that dimension made me laugh on the back of the sheet.

It seemed that she could see everything and write at the same time as everything happened. Even more as if her notes were written instantly while I performed each of the actions. The second day in Montevideo I did a city tour, we passed through the centenary stadium that I always wanted to meet since I was a child, I was a Uruguayan football fan, I imagined in the future bringing my children to watch a match of the Charrúa claw and also I imagined her screaming like crazy. I once dreamed that I had a daughter and was of golden curls like her. This was a strange combination because she could never return here, because she no longer lived and yet I felt her. And once she guessed my thought.

"Imagine you and I in a match of your claw charrúa, it would be a dream to live it, with a Pilsner beer and you taking care of a pretty girl with blond curls hehe."

Prague August 8, 2018.

That day at night I traveled to Amsterdam as a stopover to get to Prague. This city that hundreds of people had told me was a paradise. A paradise that I always wanted to know, that's why I shaped one of my most beautiful stories in it. They were too many hours of flight, and all the time thinking about her, in her tastes, in her childhood, in her loves, heck and even began to think about such nonsense, it was so much my despair to find out about her that I hired an internet package to be able to connect from the plane and find some information about her life. I sent emails to her father to tell me more about her, he was the best person to describe her, he knew her better than anyone else in the world.

I searched Google with her name for everything I could find too. I began to review their social networks from beginning to end, their photos, their comments on other walls and those of their friends on hers, events she attended during her participation in the networks, closest friends, family registered on Facebook , personal videos, photos tagged by other friends, her sites of interest, her favorite books among which there were several of mine obviously, places she visited, schools where she studied, classmates in each generation, favorite movies. Everyone turned to see me upset because they tried to sleep and I kept laughing out loud with each one of their occurrences, I saw those images on her Facebook again and again and it was another thunderous laugh. She was also a fan of the Cruz Azul! Considered the most losing team in Mexico and probably in the world, ten consecutive finals consecutively endorsed him, I did not stop laughing until the annoying flight attendant required me to respect the dream of the other passengers.

I imagined everyone together, she, me and our children, singing at the Cruz Azul stadium. Finally, the songs were like those of the Uruguayan national team "*Soyyy, celesteee, celesteeee, soy celesteeee.*" We arrived in Amsterdam and waited there for a few hours, I remembered that photo of her surrounded by beautiful tulips of all colors. I thought to return one day to take that photo that would be pending in our album.

"If you are thinking of returning one day to Amsterdam to take a picture like the one I have in my house, I want to tell you not to waste your time, that beautiful city brings me very good memories and they are not from you, so you better dedicate yourself to yours hehe."

This time her comments did not make me laugh, on the contrary I was a little upset, maybe I was jealous of not being important to her in that city, so I even thought about making a novel in that place and without thinking of her as revenge. The flight to Prague was very fast, I was finally in the land of the great Frank Kafka. The famous writer who published "Metamorphosis", a classic of a whole generation, that of peace and love. Personally, I never liked him but for my uncle that I adored, it was his passion, even when I was on Czech land, I discovered that Kafka was not born there worse, however, this country had adopted him.

The indications were almost the same, that my novel performed the dance of Prague, and it was just like that because the ghost of that Prague's girl that the protagonist imagines in every corner of this beautiful city is the same as I did reminding her that It was a ghost in my life, I decided to get drunk with Becherovka the typical drink I met online to write my novel. Being in that Czech bar I also tried the lemon flavor Bechrovka and it fascinated me.

I got drunk while walking through those cobbled streets and crossed that bridge that at the end had that magic number from when the clock was built and coincidentally it was their date and my birthday date together, what coincidences of life, or maybe everything was already predestined.

"I know that your fascination is beer so you won't resist the temptation to drink Czech beer, but we also toast with Becherovka, what's more, we drink one and one, finally I will hardly get drunk and see how you fall drunk thinking about me, while I continue drinking and enjoying the typical music with the accordion."

People laughed to see me toast with her with that giant glass full of delicious and frothy black beer thinking I was drunk seeing visions, which was also true.

I hope you do not touch the cielito lindo with the accordion because you will leave the Mexicans as drunk hehe.

And said and done, the man of the accordion began to sing the cielito lindo and many shouted ¡Viva Mexico! And I didn't mind leaving my countrymen wrong, all I thought at the time was how it was possible not to have met her before. When I left the bar, I saw that building that looks like a couple dancing and I imagined it was her and me, it is an urban legend, that drinking too much makes a couple dance there.

Florence, Italy. August 10, 2018.

And in the end with a huge hangover thinking of an incredible and ghostly woman, who had appeared in my life as the protagonist of "The dance of Prague", I took the flight to Florence.

Florence impacts you from the moment you touch that beautiful ground. I had only seen photos of that cathedral in the house of Zai and I found it impressive, but seeing it face to face in a real way, it was a magical moment, that majestic building perplexed me, and even more when I thought about my novel of "Yesterday" . I understood why there was the ideal wedding of the protagonists of the story. I even imagined that I was there with her and I took the classic photo she and I with the cathedral in the background and I thought maybe also here would be my ideal wedding. And again, I imagined her walking through that beautiful mosaic of the imposing Florence Cathedral.

"In the distance that strange combination of green, white and pink creates a unique effect on the color of that temple, you'll never see anything like it, at least that's how I weighed when I saw it in front of me. There will be our photo of that wedding that you and I will never carry out, that photo you have not seen, my dad has it stored in his closet, so you take the photo on the altar as you like and we will see that it coincides with which I took some time ago, with the help of technology you can make a

photo montage and similar that we were getting married there."

I drank a bottle of Italian wine, slowly savoring every drop dripping down my tongue and throat, imagining the excitement of that link to feel the heat caused by the fermented grape, I wrote the name on a napkin that I kept in my shirt bag because I thought it was delicious, the most delicious that I had tasted and it was in a cafeteria outside the cathedral framed the moment, until night fell and with it felt a fairly mild climate, even when it was summer, imagine that cold wind was her brushing my skin.

When I arrived at the hotel, I fell on my bed and didn't know more about myself.

- Zai, what are you doing here?

- You asked me to come.

- Yes, but you're dead, what else I want you to be here with me and to have met you.

- You are knowing me now.

She took my cheeks between her fingers and gave me a very tender kiss and settled on the other side of the bed, so I did the same. She hugged me from behind and so we stayed until dawn, her chest touching my back.

The fear that I felt at first because of her supernatural presence, dissipated when I felt her hot body touching mine, perhaps because I imagined feeling her icy hands, but they did not heat mine all night.

I woke up and looked for her everywhere, I didn't even go anywhere that day thinking that maybe she had gone out and would come back, hopefully thinking that she hadn't died and maybe everything was an invention of her, I was dying to meet her, she had that hope that she never dies even in the most illogical situations like this. Finally, I concluded that it had been a beautiful dream, although it had been perhaps the most real one, I had, I felt her arms surrounding my body so real and her chest warming my back all night.

I lost that whole day waiting for her, so I prepared to plan the next day that was the last of this strange but magical tour I was living. I also took the opportunity to write some lines on my computer about what this trip left me learning. The words flowed even more when I realized that if all my illogical and incredible fantasies lived in the last hours could be real, that was our honeymoon, our wedding night.

"There are millions of incredible people in the world and we will miss the pleasure of meeting them. I wish there was an oral memory of those fascinating people that we cannot touch with our own hands, a legacy as well as the one that Zaida Sofía had left in each of her works and even after death she had left me a great learning: although people get away and just die, you can always

live through other people as she was perhaps doing right now with every feeling I had. But above all, he had shown me that someone can be rejoiced despite any obstacle, that there was no limit to make many people happy regardless of limitations."

I turned off my computer and went to bed.

The next day I toured the rest of the important monuments of Florence and ate a delicious pasta with a lot of wine, in my life I had tasted something as delicious as Italian wine. She recommended me one in particular and it was the best option of all that I had tried, I still remember that indication and my skin bristles.

"When tasting that wine you will feel that it is my lips that you are touching in that subtle bitter and sweet taste of the grape, so my lips know so you did not have to have tried them to know how they were in life, they simply know the Merlot red wine that Run through the corners of your lips at this precise moment. "

And so, I did, to imagine for every sip I gave to that bottle of wine, my skin changed, shuddered to the point that at the end of the bottle I felt somewhat excited with that elixir. And read those lines again to return it. Imagine in each sip your lips so much that my skin bristled. There were not many pages left in that book that compiled all the indications she had given me, I felt too sad to know that soon I would have nothing new from her, everything I could experience with her seemed to die in the next few hours. Even a little scared I felt when I thought about the moment, I wouldn't know more about her. I had become too fond of his way of being or his way of writing, rather, that he had spent the best vacations of my life. As I turned to a fuller sheet, his words came to mind

"Something I loved about your novels were your poems that are necessarily related in each story."

And I asked myself, what would be your favorite poetry of all those that appear in my novels?

I was absorbed when I started reading the beginning of the next indication sheet.

"Sometimes I hate those long empty spaces in my mind, between one thought and another, because when my mind is free and no thought lurks, you automatically appear ...In case at some point you wonder what was my favorite poetry in your novels, it is this, which I am almost certain you did not write to your ex-girlfriend in the novel of "Always you", so at this moment you can be honest don't worry, I'll take your secret to the grave, heh, heh, heh. Tell me the name of the lucky one to whom you dedicated those words."

Her cunning was incredible in order to deduce my behavior at every moment. I lay on the bed in the same position with which a couple of days before I had dreamed of her, but now I was the one who hugged her touching my chest with her back and with my lips near her ear I whispered the name of that woman who had inspired that beautiful poetry. The most ironic thing is that at that moment every word of that short stanza adjusted precisely to the moment I was living in that moment and not to the past, since those empty spaces in my mind, between one thought and another, when my mind was free, after this wonderful trip with her, Zaida Sofía always appeared in my mind automatically. I packed my bags with much regret, I had completely complied with her instructions, I had also had a rather unusual holiday, but the happiness was over. Now I had to go back before I went crazy to think of her, to think of someone I had not met and would not return, and yet I was hungry to want to know more about her, and what to say about touching her lips, that would be a dream that obsessed me when I had to reach it wherever I had gone after her death. And when I was about to leave someone knocked on the door of my room. I opened and was an employee with a hotel uniform, he spoke to me in Italian, so I didn't understand absolutely anything he was trying to tell me. So, he just handed me a sealed gray envelope, which I thought contained the check out and my bill, withdrew with a smile and corresponded. I broke the envelope and was surprised once again, it was another letter from her and these seemed to be now yes, the last indications. Reading that letter and thinking that it was perhaps the last thing she had written for me, I burst into tears, with a very strange feeling, it seemed love, but who feels love for someone just by reading her words on sheets written with her letter? It seemed that I was afraid of losing touch with that person, but how could I feel afraid of losing someone with whom I never spent a moment by her side?

I was so overwhelmed with feelings and emotions that I was terrified to finish reading every letter of that present and to know that this platonic romance was over. Especially since there is no love more impossible than loving someone who no longer and will never return. I also felt helplessness that made me angry that I couldn't fight for their love and have any hope, hope in this case did not exist.

"This is my last letter to you Juanma, you must have made a gesture of relief just imagine it ha ha ha. You must be fed up of having to be following directions from someone you don't even remember, from someone you inspired in many ways. Which? When I read Psicoaffaire I thought you were a sexual patient ha ha ha, and when I read the second part of the story I confirmed it ha ha ha ha ha ha. You have no idea how I am dying of laughter at this precise moment in which I am writing to you, you could not imagine it, I even spit out with the coffee that I was drinking my cedar desk that always takes care of any stain and that apparently lasts longer than me thanks to my care."

I also burst out laughing with her words that were always so spontaneous. And I also felt her laughter in my ears in such a real way.

"However, I will not limit myself to telling you that this sickly love story fascinated me and the end did not wait for me, it changes the whole perspective of the novel from one volume to another, just as, perhaps, it changed your perspective towards me these days. I will reveal something to you, but after reading this letter you will have to burn it, it is part of the indications, otherwise you will come every night to frighten you until you cause a heart attack and you reach me from this side ha ha ha, I trust your word of man Juanma do not disappoint me, you are a gentleman and gentlemen have no memory."

At times I thought about breaking that indication so I could see it every night in whatever way it was to never lose it.

"I confess that the night I finished reading it I imagined you, yes, that night when I was with my boyfriend in the privacy I imagined that I was with you, I know that this revelation sounds quite sick, but it is part of the magic that literature achieves , imagine so many nice things."

At that moment when she stopped writing about this matter, I despaired that I could not know more details about that virtual meeting we had, so doubts killed me. How could I have imagined? Would you have liked it? Would it have been better than having me in a real way?

Would you have liked to imagine me more than being with your boyfriend without thinking of me? How many times did she imagine me and not him? What a torment to never find the answers to these questions.

"Your novel "Aleph: The myth" made me think of all the mysterious events to solve in life and that everyone will do it in the best way he pleases. When I read "Kiam" I believed in your theory that love can achieve even the unthinkable, it was perhaps at that moment that I began to think of one day being able to meet you even though I was no longer here and enjoy your company. Create a star of us as in the novel. I was fascinated by your description of Montevideo, but above all I was fascinated to be there and imagine that I was watching Kiam from that place in the universe, watching the hours and the sunset of Montevideo, drinking a cheap wine from Mendoza that I bought in a corner stall , looking back at the moon."

Her words had me hypnotized, so before I continued reading and then left the room to take a taxi to the airport, I uncovered that small bottle of complimentary wine placed on the table near the window overlooking the city center, to feel that we were drinking together and chatting, that this was not a monologue, but our last meeting.

"In your story of "The dance of Prague", I felt that this trip was done together, unfortunately I had to do it alone

and already sick with this uncomfortable guest, although with that challenge I considered leaving you very precise each of the indications so that you will enjoy as much as I am doing right now from the same bar where you will drink dark Czech beer in Wenceslas Square. I also got drunk on Becherovka until I lost my mind while watching the full moon in Prague and refraining from taking my medications for that night, which inexplicable the next day felt better than ever. Reading "Divine" for the second time made me recover my faith in God that I had abandoned because of this disease that I thought I did not deserve, however that way of knowing that at the end of everything, God will always grant everything that our faith desires, made me just ask him to give me the time to finish planning well to meet you right now, after death, and to achieve every purpose I imagined. And if you are reading this letter, it is because that was the case and my faith made it possible for us to be together all these moments in which we have traveled through the places that you ventured to know with each of your novels. And well, finally, there goes the last indication that I want you to fulfill, my biggest dream since I fell in love with your way of writing, since I found great empathy with the way you describe each thing in your works. I never thought that was possible, but it was. You were my platonic love the last years of my life, living in my imagination an alternate life, parallel to mine, one that made me forget my problems and ailments. One that made me glimpse walking with you in each of your stories, being the protagonists of all. Well, our story is finally over! It has been a pleasure to share with you these moments where I do not know where I will be and I do not have the slightest idea of how it will be, but just to think that at this moment you are remembering me it gives me enough courage to face my destiny, you calmed down with your novels and with the assurance that I have that you will follow my indications the fear that I could feel from stopping living. Rest assured that when you finish reading this letter, I do not know how I will do it, but I will give you a strong signal that I have felt the same as you during these last weeks. It is more in these moments that I know it will be the last time you think of me, I am a sea of tears, but happy that you have been with me."

I was also a sea of tears, even my glass fell to the floor staining the carpet of how weak and sad I felt, but I regained strength to reach the end and I filled the glass of wine again to be drunk at that time as she was doing it when her hands wrote for me.

What is the way to immortalize something? Publishing it! I want you to make a novel of us, of this story that we just lived. Well, that if you agree. I would love to remain there always in the physical role of this novel, see my name next to yours and that hundreds of years pass, and we continue their despite whatever. It may be another novel for you, but in my case, it will be to achieve my immortality. I thank you in advance to capture our adventure these weeks. I have nothing left to say, Mr.

Writer, that I admire you very much. I did it since I read you for the first time. And even more when you tried to flirt in the presentation of "Yesterday" and obviously I did not answer that flirt because I was already engaged, but well maybe in another life we can agree as in "Always you" and be very happy in many lives. I wish you all the success in the world and immense happiness.

Kisses.

P.S. I have left with my father a very valuable present for me, you will know whether to accept it or not.

Arrivederci, loves you:

Zaida Sofia."

I kept crying with a feeling so strong, like that cry of a child who even drowns by collapsing despair, crying, helplessness and pain. When I finished reading her farewell, the telephone in the room rang for several seconds. I didn't want to answer but I wiped away my tears and lifted my handset waiting to hear that my taxi was ready to take me to the airport.

- Hello, is anyone there?

- Goodbye

- Say, who is there, answer me. - Only that whisper was heard that I heard very clearly and was unmistakably the voice that I had heard in those videos that his father had at home.

– Answer me Zai, please!

And I didn't hear her voice again. I was shouting through that headset begging for an answer, just one more word, even a few more letters of her voice, but it was all I got.

I went down the stairs devastated, dragging my suitcase, but at the same time excited after having assumed that I had heard her sweet voice and I was delighting the landscape of the hotel at the airport with the window open to feel that cool wind that was despite being summer , the day was cloudy, I saw each building in Florence as something majestic, as well as the history that had been housed there.

I arrived at her father's house and the first thing I did was hug him tightly and cry which was contagious and in an instant, we were both wrapped in a cry of joy rather than sadness.

- I heard her, Don Ernesto, I heard her voice clearly from the hotel telephone receiver before returning.

This time I did not refuse to drink a whiskey with him, moreover, this time unlike the previous ones I was the one who proposed it.

- Tell me everything, the complete story of your vacation, son.

- Of course, but I will not do it without that delicious whiskey that you keep in the cellar to be able to express myself better.

- Express yourself better? Haha that's your master plan, I go for two glasses, how do you take it, alone or on the rocks?

- On the rocks-

Served two glasses of that whiskey that was a delight to the palate, although I only wanted to always try that wine that evoked the lips of Zaida Sofia, and from which I had brought all the bottles that were possible in my suitcase.

- Now, Mr. Writer, tell me about your experiences on your trip.

He spoke to me in a tone as if he were already part of his family. I told him all my experiences in detail, even the dream I had with her, obviously I refrained from telling him, her revelation that she had imagined being with me when she made love with her husband, that secret I would take it to the grave, however the dilemma was if I should capture it in the novel I would write about us.

We drank a couple more whiskeys, while revealing to him about my plans to make the novel with this story, without telling him that it was her will, maybe in the future I would tell him and so that book would make a better sense for him. I finished telling him those days that were almost a honeymoon for me.

- That's all- my voice was already broken by the effect of alcohol- and I just need to ask you to give me a gift she left for me with you sir.

- Don't tell me sir anymore, we're almost Juanma family.

- I appreciate that distinction although I know that I don't deserve it because there must be more close and important relatives that are always present in your mind.

- It's a distinction that can be official one day.

- Official? - If Zai came up with a lot of crazy things, I thought it was the same and it was because of her father's inheritance that she also had her own in regard to rare occurrences, it happened to me for a moment that she told me to marry her, which seemed to scratch me in madness because Zai would never return. Almost like a father forcing his daughter's boyfriend to marry her. Instead of stressing me, it made me laugh to think about that and take it as a joke in case that happened. However, the answer was something that never crossed my mind.

- Take it! - He handed me a silver colored envelope that contained some keys to access a place and the most prestigious specialty hospital logos in the country.

- What is this? - I asked him because I really didn't have the slightest idea of what the purpose of those keys was.

- Find out for yourself and when you know what it is, confirm if you agree to carry out that last wish of Zai, everything is already fixed.

It began to bother me a little that they always had everything arranged for me, as if I couldn't make decisions for myself. So, I was heading towards the exit of the house.

- Ok, Don Ernesto, I will check it at my house and call you to tell you what I think of all this.

I said goodbye to that old man who was already like my father, with a big brotherly hug.

I decided to call the hospital directly to find out what the matter was about that envelope and I took the most unexpected surprise of my life, once again Zai had left me with my mouth open, but this time I did not know if her surprise excited me or it frightened me, so many mixed feelings passed to me that perhaps the one who dominated most was my intense desire not to stop thinking about her.

- It can't be! - I shouted when I hung up that call with one of the hospital receptionists and gave her those references.

It took me a few minutes to assimilate that proposal and be able to digest some reasonable alternative. When Zai learned of her illness and that it was just beginning, she thought that the only way to have children in case she managed to beat cancer would be by freezing her eggs, before her organs could be affected by the treatment, also thinking of an option so that her father did not stay alone when he lacked his only daughter, so he imagined three scenarios. The first who managed to fight this battle and could herself through in vitro fertilization procreate frozen eggs. The second was that, along with her illness, she could find a womb that could have her baby even if she was not there, and the third one who was living at that time, her request as the writer she most admired was that I was the donor who made that dream possible after his death.

It was crazy! So many things went through my mind that day that I learned of her plans, even my headache felt the stress of so many thoughts and fears that went through my mind.

Why me? What would I feel being a parent? All these questions excited me in the first instance and then made me sad to think about the immense responsibility they involved. I didn't know whether or not to accept that strange request, it seemed very simple to just serve as a donor and disappear, but it was no longer being a donor to someone I didn't know. It was to be someone who now had a great affection, it would sound stupid but to some extent I thought I loved that person and think that if I did it I wanted to live my whole life with the fruit of this strange relationship. I always thought that everything in life is a risk, so what else did I take if I took this risk and faced responsibility, among my fear I thought that regardless of any consequence, having a child should be God's greatest blessing. I think that yearning to be a father one day would eventually overcome any doubts I had. That night I dreamed of golden curls of a beautiful girl running through the gardens of Prague. And in the end that smile appeared Zai waiting for us at home to hug us both.

I got up and drove to her home immediately, it was my last day in Culiacan, so I had to tell her father that I accepted her proposal, although he didn't know that I also had something even more crazy in mind.

He shouted with happiness when he heard me, I think that joy came over that home again, he felt the presence of Zai everywhere, knowing that a part of her could bear fruit.

- If it is a boy, how will we put him?

- Well, like you, father-in-law - his frown was annoying and then he changed it as joking.

- Ha ha ha, I'm kidding, I love the idea that you say so, that by the way are you, Mr. Writer.

- Tell me about yourself, I already appreciate you as a father.

- Ok Juanma, and if it's a girl, how will we put it?

- Obviously, Elia Sofía, like her grandmother and her mother.

That afternoon drinking whiskey I found out something else I did not know about Zai's big heart, she had decided to donate all the organs of her body that could be used despite her illness to give hope to other people.

- I will return a few days to Veracruz to see my family and wait for the necessary time that the doctors recommended me to donate. While I'm away I want you to do me a great favor. I know it sounds very complicated, but you are a very dear man in the country and very powerful, so please I beg you to investigate and tell me who were the beneficiaries of Zai's organs.

- The beneficiaries? Why Juanma?

- It is that I am writing a novel and I would like to know if I can know that information that would help me to develop some details of it - I had to lie to him so that he did not know what was going through my mind at that time.

- A novel of your story with my daughter. I think it's great, don't worry, count on it. When you return I will have that information.

- Thank you very much, you do not know how much I thank you, even if I could before I come back tell me on the phone, I would be very grateful to advance in my story.

- I will do it as soon as I have it, take it for granted.

I returned to Veracruz and drove by road to Coatzacoalcos, my homeland, thinking a thousand things on the road I wanted to do from what I had lived with Zai. That day I saw the sunset on the boardwalk, I had not seen anything more beautiful in my life so from a young age I always took that route to go to my house and when I arrived I took paper and pen and began to write some poetry. Although my boardwalk was more beautiful than the one in Montevideo, the one in my city was missing our star as in my novel "Kiam", but I already had it now, it was her.

The next day I was awakened by a call from Don Ernesto, I answered quickly and wrote down in a notebook with my pen all the information that he provided, asking him to send it by email would be complicated since Don Ernesto was not familiar with the Technology as it was logical. There was only one piece of information that I was interested in knowing and that had gotten into my head to find out since I knew she donated her organs, her eyes. The eyes are the window of the soul, so she had part of the soul of the woman who I had fallen in love with, in a couple of weeks with her spontaneous and unique way of being. I wrote down the address of that lucky girl who had regained her sight thanks to Zai's transplant received from her corneas and decided to go look for her. I could not waste more time. I drove like crazy to cross the city and reach that building of simple apartments that were in the west. I knew almost beforehand that Zai had to choose people who lived in my city, it was so surprising her way of making me feel unique, that was the most viable option.

I knocked on the door and I knew that it was she when I saw those beautiful eyes that I had only observed fleetingly without knowing her in my presentations, in my dreams and in the photos at Zai's house. I felt that flutter in my stomach when you are in love when you see the rays of Zai's gaze alive.

- Is it you Gisselle Carmona? - Yes, sir, tell me how can I help you?

- Look, I'm Juan Manuel, a family member of Zaida Sofía Torruco Stackpole, the girl who donated her corneas to you when she died, and if you don't have any problem, I'd like to talk with you for five minutes. I mean, only if you accept.

- Of course, come in. Sit in the living room, my mother is about to arrive, so just let me finish cooking dinner and in a moment, we talk, will you?

- Perfect, thank you very much here I wait.

It was a department of social interest with a very simple room but with every corner very well organized. Her gaze reminded me too much of Zai, I even felt a huge desire to kiss her, but if I tried at least I would run from her house without achieving the purpose I had gone to.

We talked for hours to get to know each other and she was such a nice person that I think what Zai had done for her was totally deserved. I was sure that she had left her essence on earth in every person with whom she had contact and in this case with Gisselle who was the one with her beautiful eyes.

- You're as nice as Zai, did you know that? - She was very serious for a moment, my comment seemed to bother her. - Sorry, if I said something that bothered you.

- No, it's not that, is that ... - She burst into tears at that moment and I could barely understand her words, but I managed to know the cause.

- Before that accident where I lost my sight I was a very different person, you have no idea of all the bad things that I did in life and the negative attitude I had even with my family, I had drug addiction problems and I was involved with groups of criminals, however after the transplant I had a new life and my mother and my family they are happy because I changed radically. I think that feeling that I would not see again changed my life. Everybody tells me that from transplant, I see the world differently.

That was what she thought, I had another theory, which was the Zai effect on her life, having her vision, I could see the world very differently.

- Can I invite you to dinner wherever you like, and we continue talking?

- Ok but wait for my mother to let her know.

- Okay.

We had dinner in my favorite place, although it was very far from home, we had the view of the sea and the reflection of the hill of San Martín on the waves with the moon, which made our first date a very romantic evening, something like that I imagined with Zai when traveling to Montevideo.

Her look was beautiful, so on a couple of occasions I called her Zai by mistake, because I felt I was with her.

- Well, after knowing almost everything about me, tell me what brought you to my house?

- First of all, I wanted to see Zai's eyes again, have something alive of her yet. - It was really the first time I saw them after our strange relationship, but I couldn't tell her that because she would realize that I didn't even know Zai and distrust me. - Second, I want to propose something, although it may seem crazy to you but I think I should try and ask for it.

- Whatever you tell me I will do, you have no idea how grateful I am with Zaida's family, in fact I planned to visit them on vacation just to raise money to travel and tell them personally.

- Look, I will speak clearly and bluntly because I don't have much time left to return to Zai's house. She left her frozen eggs so that we had a child when she was gone, by in vitro fertilization. And my proposal is that you be the womb that has that son that she so longed for.- She fell silent and her gesture became very serious.- I'm sorry to tell you this, but before you run away in horror I will tell you that for me it would be very important that you were the person that could have that baby.

In fact, she got up from the table and withdrew home alone without saying a word and without letting me accompany her back. At least I made the attempt, I stayed in that restaurant and ordered a couple of beers to have that bitter drink of shame.

After two days she called me, her voice felt quite nervous.

- I will, Juan Manuel

- How? What will you do?

- What you asked for. Thanks to the help of your girlfriend I was able to recover my life, so I will do it, the detail is that I don't have the way to get there to carry out that process you mention.

- Do not worry about that, I will cover all the expenses, next week we will travel to Culiacan to adjust details, you have no idea how happy this news makes me, and how happy Zai is wherever she is.

Now I just needed to convince Zai's father that she was the woman who would have our son and not the option he had already chosen. So, I hurried to make the donation in that clinic, I put some films of those that are in that place to motivate the donation, in each woman I saw her and it was very easy to do that process.

Leaving the clinic I went to greet Don Ernesto.

- Good afternoon, Don Ernesto.

- Don Ernesto? days ago you called me father-in-law, why so much formality now? do not tell me that you will reject Zai's last will.

- No, I would never do that, I am determined to do it and to be part of this family, only I would like to ask you a favor.

- Talk son what you need you will have it.

- I contacted Zai's cornea donor and convinced her that she was the one with that will have that baby. He was thoughtful for a moment.

- Personally, I don't think it's the best option, but if you want it that way, let's do it then, what better for me than having someone very close to Zai.

Those curls that I dreamed one day became a beautiful reality with the birth of Elia Sofia. From that moment on my life changed but even with all the happiness there was not a single day that I did not wish to have met Zaida in life.

- Grandpa are you afraid of dying?

I let out a big laugh that hurt my whole body.

- How do you think son I will finally be with her.

- With whom grandfather?

- Forget it, is a very long story that one day your grandmother Giselle will tell you. Or you can also find it in this book.

- I gave him a book from my posthumous novel making he swear that he would read it when he was already a teenager.

I closed my eyes for a moment and when I opened them, I was already in that place, the most peaceful in the world, where you breathe a very light air, and everything shone around the intensity of the light. Everything was quiet, I did not understand anything that happened until suddenly everything quickly darkened, and I saw nothing around, not even a shadow, it was total darkness, in no direction could anything be appreciated.

A terrible sense of fear began to flood me for not knowing where I was and not seeing anything around. I didn't even hear a single noise. It was scary that moment when I thought I felt abandoned in an unknown place. I was scared of the contact in my right hand with someone's skin. It was a hand and pulled me hard until I returned to the place of intense peace moments ago.

- I told you I would always be by your side.

Everything was light of an intensity that barely let me see around, I started walking.

I missed you so much, Zai.

“This novel is dedicated to those great warriors to whom God entrusted that titanic battle against Cancer”